Bed Hog

by **Georgette Noullet**

illustrated by **David Slonim**

Marshall Cavendish Children

Marshall Cavendish Corporation,
99 White Plains Road, Tarrytown, NY 10591
www.marshallcavendish.us/kids

The illustrations are rendered in acrylic
and charcoal on illustration board.

Book design by Vera Soki
Editor: Marilyn Brigham

Library of Congress Cataloging-in-Publication Data

Noullet, Georgette.
Bed hog / by Georgette Noullet ; illustrated by David Slonim. — 1st ed.
p. cm.
Summary: The family dog spends a long night looking for a
comfortable place to sleep.
ISBN 978-0-7614-5823-4
[1. Dogs—Fiction. 2. Sleep—Fiction.] I. Slonim, David, ill. II. Title.
PZ7.N85Be 2011   [E]—dc22   2010008089

Printed in China (E)
First Marshall Cavendish Pinwheel Books edition, 2011
1 3 5 6 4 2

For R.J.
—G. N.

To Bonnie, who hasn't minded me hogging
the blankets for twenty-three years
—D. S.

"Good night, son.
Good night, Bailey."

"Move over, bed hog dog."

"What's wrong, little one?"